The Crocodile's True Colors

Written and illustrated by Eva Montanari

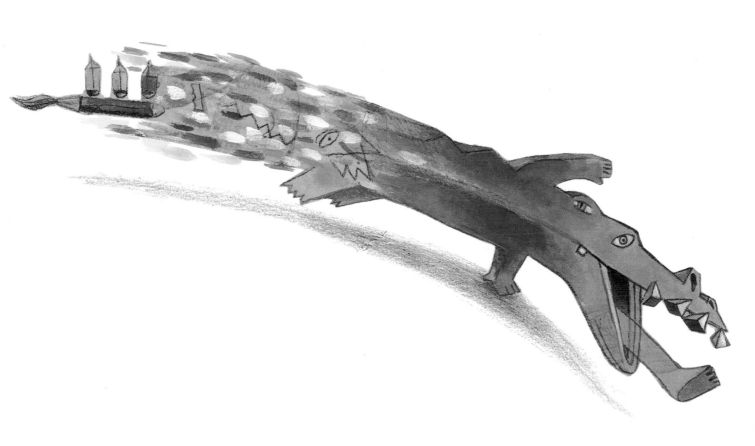

Watson-Guptill Publications/New York

In the grassy fields of Africa, there is a school where young animals learn to read and write, to make music and art.

Sometimes the animals go to the windows and look down at the river below. They watch the long tail that ripples the surface of the water. They know it belongs to the Crocodile.

*To my mother, who laughs with her hand in
front of her mouth, just like Little Monkey*

© Edizioni Arka, 2002

First published in the United States in 2002
by Watson-Guptill Publications,
a division of VNU Business Media, Inc.
770 Broadway, New York, NY 10003
www.watsonguptill.com

Library of Congress Cataloging-in-Publication Data

Montanari, Eva, 1977–
   The crocodile's true colors / written and illustrated by Eva
Montanari.
       p. cm.
Summary: In answering the young African animals' questions about the
ferocious crocodile living in the nearby river, Master Elephant also
teaches them about various forms of artistic expression.
   ISBN 0-8230-2435-0
[1. Crocodiles--Fiction. 2. Animals--Fiction. 3. Perception--Fiction.
4. Art appreciation--Fiction.] I. Title.
   PZ7.M76344
   [Cr 2002]
   [E]--dc21

                                        2001008420

ISBN: 0-8230-2435-0

First published in Italy in 2002
by Edizioni Arka, Milan

Printed in Italy

First printing, 2002

1 2 3 4 5 6 7 8 / 09 08 07 06 05 04 03 02

The little animals have heard terrible things about the Crocodile. They've heard about his powerful jaws and sharp teeth. They've heard that he can sneak up silently and eat you in the blink of an eye.

One day, while the animals are looking
down at the river, their teacher, Master
Elephant, asks, "Who'd like to paint a
picture of the Crocodile?"

"I will!" roars Little Lion.

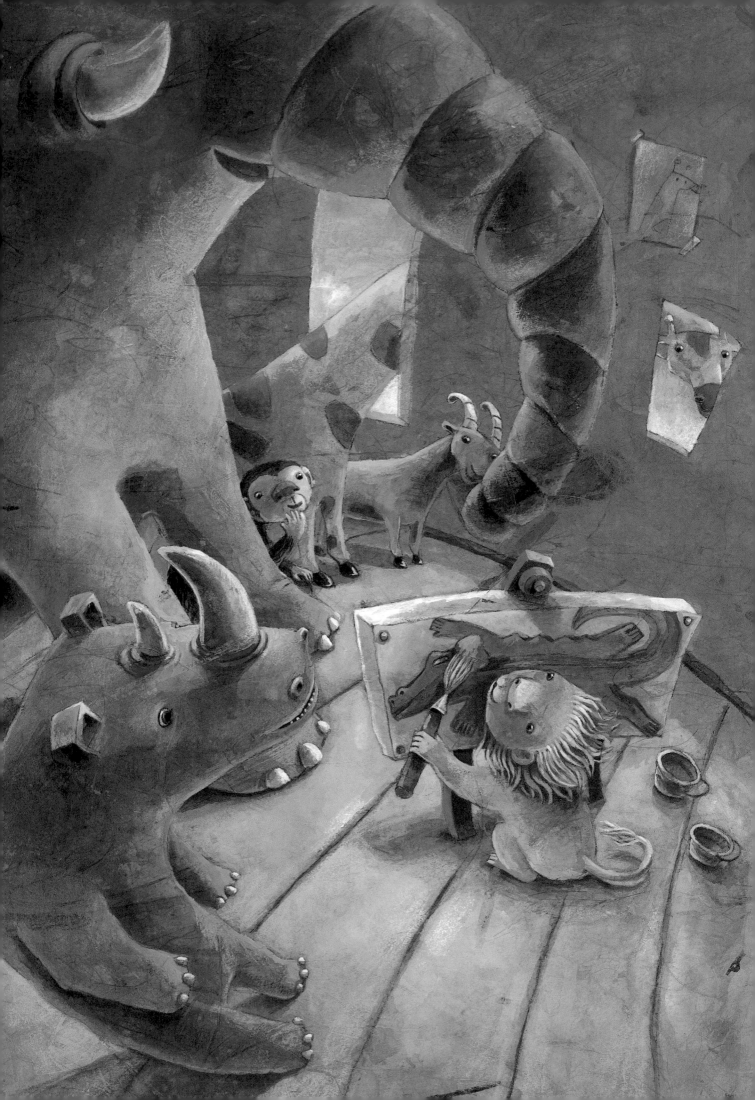

Little Lion paints a long, zigzag body with big purple strokes. "My father says the Crocodile is the most ferocious creature on earth!" he roars.

"Ha ha!" the other animals laugh. "The Crocodile isn't *purple*!" Little Monkey laughs hardest of all.

"Little Lion has painted the Crocodile he's afraid of," says Master Elephant. "He has used color to show how he feels. In painting, this is called *Expressionism*."

Little Rhinocerous decides to go next. "My mother says that the Crocodile has pointed teeth and swallows fish whole!" He paints the Crocodile with scales that look like pyramids, and with both eyes on one side of its head. "If I could see the Crocodile from below, I'd see his tummy, and maybe the fish he just ate," he says.

"Ha ha!" the other animals laugh. "That doesn't even look like a real animal!" Little Monkey laughs the longest.

"Little Rhinocerous has shown the Crocodile as if we could see him from all sides at once, including the inside," says Master Elephant. "In painting, this is called *Cubism.*"

Now Little Gazelle wants to try. "My sister says the Crocodile can eat you in a flash! He swims so fast that just when you think you see him he's already gone." She uses short brushstrokes to show the Crocodile running off the canvas onto the wall.

"Ha ha!" laugh the animals. "Your Crocodile doesn't even have a body!" Little Monkey rolls on the floor, hooting away.

"Little Gazelle has shown how the Crocodile moves," says Master Elephant. "She's shown the past, the present, and the future, all at the same time. In painting, this is called *Futurism*."

Little Giraffe goes next. "My uncle says the Crocodile has jaws full of teeth that can snap you in half, no matter how big you are!" Soon her canvas is filled with wild spots, dots, and lines in crazy colors.

"Ha ha!" laugh the animals. "Your painting just looks like a bunch of scribbles!" As usual, Little Monkey laughs the hardest.

"Little Giraffe has painted shapes and colors that aren't supposed to look like the real Crocodile," says Master Elephant. "They are meant to show a feeling about him. In painting, this is called *Abstractionism.*"

"Okay," says Master Elephant, pointing his long trunk at Little Monkey, "how about *you* taking a turn?"

Little Monkey grabs a canvas and starts gluing
things onto it: pencil shavings, a compass, a
paintbrush—all sorts of things.

"Ha ha!" laugh the other animals. "That
isn't even a real painting!"

"Little Monkey has picked things at random for his painting," says Master Elephant. "The objects don't mean anything, they are just meant to surprise you. We call this kind of art *Dada*."

"What does *Dada* mean?" asks Little Giraffe.

"It's a nonsense word," says Master Elephant. "It's meant to poke fun at serious words, just like Little Monkey's art pokes fun at serious paintings."

Little Monkey isn't laughing anymore. In fact, he's hopping
mad that no one likes his painting. He starts throwing books
and paint all over the place. Jars of color fly out the window,
staining the river purple, red, blue, and yellow.

Suddenly, a long body comes to the surface of the water.
"The Crocodile!" gasps Little Giraffe.

The animals watch as the Crocodile dashes out of the river and into the baobab trees, leaving a trail of purple, red, blue, and yellow footprints behind. He doesn't look very ferocious. . . .

Master Elephant smiles. "I wonder what the Crocodile's true colors are? I wonder whether he's good or bad?"

"Can't you tell us?" asks Little Monkey.
"Well!" says Master Elephant. "Purple or turquoise, cube-shaped or made with squiggles, all I know is that each and every one of us sees things in our own unique way. And I wonder," he laughs, "how the Crocodile sees *us*?"

From among the baobab trees, Little Crocodile stares back at the animals in the school. Master Crocodile has told him stories about the Lion whose roar can be heard across water, the Elephant whose footsteps make the ground shake, the Giraffe who is as tall as the sky.

But isn't that the Lion smiling at him? he wonders. And now the Giraffe, too? Little Crocodile smiles back. Then he tries to look ferocious. After all, he *is* a crocodile.